*B*eth March would do just about anything to help someone in need. She's kindhearted, loyal, and caring. So when she catches scruffy Sean O'Neill stealing apples from Aunt March's garden, Beth listens to the hungry boy's sad story. She's moved when she hears that Sean's widowed mother and younger siblings are immigrants from poverty-stricken Ireland. But times are hard in Massachusetts, too. Sean's mother has been ill and out of work, and with sisters and brothers to care for, Sean has had to scrape up food for them any way he can. Promising to help, Beth gives him whatever food and old clothes her family can spare. It's not enough, and Beth makes a plan to steal from wealthy Aunt March. But Sean's own thieving forces Beth to question what being a true friend really means—and together they discover generosity in the person who has seemed the most coldhearted.

PORTRAITS
of LITTLE WOMEN

Beth Makes
a Friend

Don't miss any of the
Portraits of Little Women

PORTRAITS
of LITTLE WOMEN

*Beth Makes
a Friend*

Susan Beth Pfeffer

DELACORTE PRESS

Published by
Delacorte Press
Bantam Doubleday Dell Publishing Group, Inc.
1540 Broadway
New York, New York 10036

Library of Congress Cataloging-in-Publication Data

Pfeffer, Susan Beth.
  Portraits of little women. Beth makes a friend / Susan Beth Pfeffer.
      p.   cm.
  Based on characters found in Louisa May Alcott's Little women.
  Summary: Beth tries to help an impoverished Irish immigrant boy and
his family by stealing a silver bowl from her great-aunt and giving it to
the O'Neills to sell.
  ISBN 0-385-32583-5
  [1. Poor—Fiction. 2. Stealing—Fiction. 3. Great-aunts—Fiction.
4. Immigrants—Fiction. 5. Irish Americans—Fiction.] I. Alcott, Louisa
May, 1832–1888. Little women. II. Title.
PZ7.P44855Pj   1998
[Fic]—dc21   97-27847
                                                         CIP
                                                          AC

The text of this book is set in 13-point Cochin.

Cover and text design by Patrice Sheridan
Cover illustration copyright © 1998 by Lori Earley
Text illustrations copyright © 1998 by Marcy Ramsey
Activities illustrations copyright © 1998 by Laura Maestro

Manufactured in the United States of America

April 1998

10 9 8 7 6 5 4 3 2 1

BVG

FOR ROZ AND STEVE SHAW

CONTENTS

CHAPTER 1

"Beth! Are you ready yet?"

"Coming, Marmee," ten-year-old Beth March said with a sigh. She was still in the bedroom she shared with her younger sister, Amy. Amy was out visiting friends, and Beth's oldest sister, Meg, was doing errands. Only Jo, Beth's next older sister, and Beth remained in the house.

"Poor Bethy," Jo said. "Having to pay a courtesy call on Aunt March."

"I don't mind," Beth said, but Jo laughed.

"Of course you do," said Jo. "We all do, except maybe Amy, who can see past Aunt March herself and admire all her possessions."

"Beth!"

"I'd better go," Beth said, sighing again. It was unlike her to keep Marmee waiting, but she would do almost anything to avoid visiting Aunt March.

"Don't let her scare you," Jo said. "Just remember to be polite and sweet." She paused for a moment. "But you're always polite and sweet," she said. "I'm the one who has to remember to be." She laughed.

Beth would have laughed too if she hadn't so dreaded the next couple of hours. Instead she went downstairs, where she found Marmee standing impatiently by the front door.

"Really, Beth," Marmee said. "You act as though you've never met Aunt March. She's no one to be shy about."

"I'm not shy about her," Beth said, which was the truth. She was terrified of Aunt March, a feeling that was considerably stronger than simple shyness. Sometimes Beth had awful dreams, in which Aunt March turned into a tiger or a lion or some equally dreadful animal Beth had seen pictures of, and got into the March house and threatened to eat them all alive. Beth told herself the real Aunt March was nowhere near as bad, but in her heart she didn't quite believe that.

Aunt March was Father's aunt by marriage. Beth hardly remembered Uncle March, but everyone agreed he had been a very pleasant man. No one said his widow was pleasant. Aunt March was one of the great ladies of Concord, where the March family lived. Beth knew she wasn't the only one frightened of the old woman.

But Aunt March was family, and that meant the March girls had to pay their respects to her. Meg didn't seem to mind, and as Jo had pointed out, Amy almost liked visiting Aunt March. Jo was more bored by their great-aunt than frightened. But they were all braver than Beth, and none of them had had dreams in which Aunt March ate them alive.

It was a long walk to Aunt March's house. Marmee and Beth chatted as they walked, talking about the latest litter of kittens in the neighborhood (Beth had her eye on a particularly fetching calico) and what the girls would do when the new school year began. Beth knew Marmee was coming up with subjects to ~~keep Beth from thinking about what lay~~ ahead. It almost worked, too.

"Hello, Williams," Marmee said to Aunt March's butler when they finally reached the house. "Will you please tell Mrs. March that my daughter and I are here?"

"Certainly, ma'am," Williams replied. Beth was relieved to see him go. Her family had one servant, Hannah, who kept the house and did the cooking. Aunt March had so many servants, Beth had long since stopped trying to remember their names. They seemed to come and go at a fairly steady clip.

Williams came back and ushered them into Aunt March's back parlor. Beth felt a bit relieved, since the back parlor was less formal than the front one. She wasn't the sort of girl who broke things, but at Aunt March's house she always felt as if she were.

Aunt March exchanged cold kisses with Marmee and Beth. She told them to sit down, and they did.

"What a terrible day," Aunt March said.

"Oh, dear," said Marmee. "Why?"

"I've had to dismiss yet another servant," Aunt March replied. "This one carried on such a flirtation with the undergardener that neither one of them was getting any work done."

"It can be a problem finding good help," Marmee said.

Hannah, Beth knew, had been with her family since before Meg was born. But Marmee knew lots of people, and they must have told her of their trials with servants.

"They always say to hire young girls," Aunt March said, "since they don't have any encumbrances. But they do seem determined to create encumbrances at the first opportunity."

"Young girls *will* fall in love," Marmee said. "Did you dismiss the undergardener as well?"

"I was tempted to," Aunt March replied. "But my gardener is overworked as it is, and he simply refused to hear of it. That is how my life is. My decisions are dictated to me by my servants."

Beth glanced around the room. She was accustomed to Hannah's telling her what to do and couldn't work up much sympathy for Aunt March in her dilemma. Instead she looked at Aunt March's things. And Aunt March certainly had plenty of things to look at. Even in the back parlor, there were silver ornaments and fine old paintings and little china figurines. Beth's house was decorated mostly with books and with the paintings Amy made. Of course, Beth's house had a piano and Aunt March's didn't, and that made Beth's house far nicer, in her opinion.

"Beth!" Aunt March said. "Beth!" And she actually clapped her hands to get Beth's attention.

"Oh, excuse me," Beth said, shaken from her thoughts. "Did you say something?"

"Has no one taught you to listen to your

elders?" Aunt March said. "I do declare, children today are brought up with no manners whatsoever."

"I'm sorry, Aunt March," Beth said. She was too. The last thing she wanted was to have Aunt March focus her attention on her.

"If you had chosen to listen to me, you would have heard me ask you if you wanted to go to the orchard and pick some apples for your sisters and yourself," Aunt March said. "But I suppose your very lack of interest means you wouldn't care to do it."

"Oh, no," Beth said. "I'd love to leave you. I mean, I'd love to be outdoors. No, what I really mean is thank you, Aunt March. I know my sisters would truly enjoy the apples."

Beth could see Marmee trying hard not to laugh. Beth didn't dare look too hard at Aunt March to see what she was doing.

"Very well," Aunt March said. "Ask Bertha for a basket for the apples. No, not Bertha. I had to let her go last week. Oh, ask Williams to get one for you. He's loyal to me, at least. Then go to the orchard and gather the apples.

We have an abundant crop this year, and I'm sure I won't miss any you might take."

"Thank you, Aunt March," Beth said, far more grateful to Aunt March for being allowed outdoors than for any apples she might gather.

CHAPTER 2

*A*unt March's house stood on a large plot of land. Much of it was devoted to gardens of vegetables that were used for her own table, and of beautiful flowers that decorated her home. She also had grapevines and apple orchards. It was to the orchards that Beth gratefully strolled.

Jo, she knew, would somehow climb a tree in spite of her voluminous skirts, but Beth decided to be satisfied with grabbing apples off low-hanging branches and finding unbruised ones on the ground. Her family had an apple tree, but it bore winter apples. Aunt March had summer apple trees, and her apples were ripe and would make for good eating.

The sun was shining, and a few fluffy clouds floated across the blue sky. A slight breeze kept the day from being too hot. Beth couldn't imagine better weather, but she would have been happy enough picking apples in midwinter if it kept her from having to talk with Aunt March.

She began by picking apples off low-hanging branches and carefully putting them in the basket Williams had gotten for her. After she had picked eight or ten, she turned her attention to the ones lying on the ground. The longer she took, the less time she'd have to spend indoors, so each apple seemed to demand a thorough examination. A little bruise here, a wormhole there. Beth put those apples back on the ground and kept looking for just the right ones. Apples worthy of her sisters, she thought, and then she laughed. Her sisters were accustomed to cutting away the bruises and the wormholes. But they too would be fussy if it meant they could avoid Aunt March.

As she continued her search, Beth became aware of a rustling in one of the trees. She was sure it was a bird, but she thought it might be a special sort. An eagle, perhaps, or some exotic bird that might have escaped from someone's home. Beth didn't think peacocks flew, but it was worth looking up to see.

It took a few moments to discover from just which tree the noise had come. Beth wasn't sure she would have found it, except that the rustling started up again. It was hard to look up with the sun shining so brightly and the branches of the trees dark against the light. But Beth shielded her eyes with her hand, and after some searching she found the source of the noise.

It wasn't a bird at all. It was a boy, hiding in the branches of one of the trees.

"What are you doing there?" Beth asked. Normally she would have been far too frightened to speak, but she was startled. And there

was something comical about the sight of a boy cowering in the branches.

"And who are you to be asking?" the boy responded.

"I'm Beth March," said Beth. "My great-aunt lives here. She invited me to pick some apples. Who are you?"

"I'm no great-nephew of such a fine lady," the boy said. "I'll grant you that."

"Why don't you come down?" Beth asked. "I won't hurt you."

"As though I was worried about a little slip of a thing such as you," the boy said. "Watch your head. Some apples might fall down along with me."

Beth inched away from the tree. Sure enough, some apples fell as the boy climbed down.

"Oh," Beth said as she got a good look at the boy. He was about her height and very thin, with bright red hair, freckles sprinkled across his face, and the greenest eyes she'd ever seen. His clothes were hardly better than rags, and he had no shoes.

"You are the fine lady, aren't you?" the boy said.

"Who, me?" Beth asked. "I try to be a lady, but I'm hardly fine."

The boy snorted. "Look at you," he said. "Fancy dress. Pretty ribbons. Every inch the lady."

Beth looked down at her blue gingham dress, a hand-me-down first from Meg, who took good care of her clothing, and then from Jo, who was far less tidy. "It's patched," she said. "Marmee fixed it, but she did it so well you can hardly see. And the ribbons were Christmas presents. And you still haven't told me your name or what you were doing in Aunt March's apple tree."

"And what does it look like I was doing?" the boy asked. He took a big bite out of an apple and then proceeded to devour it. He stared at Beth as though defying her to stop him.

"It looks as if you were picking apples," Beth said. "But Aunt March didn't tell me to expect anyone out here."

"And would I be likely to be asking the grand lady's permission," the boy asked, "when these apples are here waiting for the likes of me?"

"You were taking Aunt March's apples?" Beth asked. "That's stealing. That's a sin."

"And it's a sin for me to be so hungry," the boy said. "So it's a choice of sins, and I picked thieving as the lesser one."

"Well, if you're hungry, I'm sure it would be fine for you to eat an apple," Beth said. "You could go to the house and ask Aunt March to give you some food. Use her kitchen door, though. I'm not sure Williams would let you in."

"And who is Williams to be turning me down?" the boy asked.

"He's Aunt March's butler," Beth said. "He's really very nice, but I think you would startle him."

"I'll not be asking a butler for charity," the boy said. "Nor a fine lady, either. These apples are God's gift to us all, and I'll just be taking my share."

"If you need help, I'd think you'd be grateful for it," Beth said. "What is your name, anyway, and where are you from? You don't talk like anyone I know."

"And that's because the folks here all have the same flat voices," the boy said. "Where I'm from we sing when we speak."

"It must be very musical there," Beth said. "Do you play the piano?"

"We wouldn't be owning one of those," the boy said, taking a final bite from the apple and tossing the core under a tree. "My name is Sean O'Neill, and it's from County Limerick I hail."

"Is that in Massachusetts?" Beth asked.

"Ireland," the boy said.

"Ireland?" Beth said. "That's in Europe."

"I suppose so," Sean said. "It's certainly not in Massachusetts."

"How long have you been here?" Beth asked. "In Massachusetts, I mean."

"Too long," Sean replied. "Long enough to know it's as heartless a land as the one we left. Long enough for my clothes to turn to rags.

16

Long enough for my father to die, and then my wee sister, and my mother to weep tears enough to fill the ocean."

"I'm so sorry," Beth said. "Please tell me what I can do to help."

Sean stared at her. "And it's help you're offering?" he said. "I thought for sure it would be the jail for stealing such a fine apple."

"Oh, no," Beth said. "I just thought maybe you didn't realize you were stealing it, that's all."

"I know all about thieving," the boy said. "I've been taught right from wrong."

"Beth! Beth! It's time to go!"

"That's Marmee," Beth said to Sean. But instead of replying, the boy grabbed the basket Beth had filled with apples and ran out of Aunt March's orchard.

"Stop!" Beth cried, but Sean ignored her. Beth sighed. Sean might know right from wrong, but he seemed to have them mixed up.

CHAPTER 3

"What do you plan to tell Aunt March about the basket?" Jo asked Beth the next day as they strolled through town. Marmee had asked them to go to the general store and pick up some flour Hannah needed for baking. Beth had spent their time together telling Jo all about Sean O'Neill.

"I don't know," Beth said. "I've been thinking perhaps I could buy another basket and she wouldn't know hers had been stolen."

"Baskets are expensive," Jo said. "Where would you get the money?"

"I could save it," Beth said. "I have fifty

cents. How much do you think a basket costs?"

"I'm not sure," Jo replied. "But it doesn't seem fair that you should have to use your fifty cents to replace a basket that a boy stole from you."

"No," said Beth. "It doesn't really seem fair to me either. But Jo, you should have seen what he was wearing. Hannah wouldn't even clean with rags as frayed as his. And he ate that apple as though he hadn't eaten anything in days."

"Still, stealing is wrong, and I don't like to see you be the one to have to pay for it," Jo said. "I'm sure if you told Aunt March the truth, she'd know what to do about it."

Beth shook her head. "She'd probably insist on finding Sean and having him sent to jail," she said. "And I don't think he was really stealing the basket, just the apples that were in it. Besides, I wouldn't have the courage to tell Aunt March the truth. So I might as well see if I can find a basket that costs only fifty cents."

"I have twenty-five cents," Jo said. "You can have it if you need it."

"Thank you," Beth said, and gave Jo's hand a squeeze. Beth knew she shouldn't have a favorite sister, but she felt a closeness to Jo that was different from her feelings for anybody else. And she knew Jo felt it in return, which only made it sweeter.

As they were about to enter the store, Beth looked down the street and saw a boy with bright red hair about a hundred feet away. "Jo, that's him," Beth whispered. "That's Sean."

"Are you sure?" Jo asked loudly enough that the boy turned to face them. He took one look and then began to run away.

"I'll catch him," Jo said, "and make him give Aunt March's basket back!" She began to chase Sean.

Beth watched for a moment, then trotted after them. Sean ran slowly at first, apparently not worried that a girl could catch him. But he had underestimated Jo, who was known as the fastest runner in Concord. When he saw that she was catching up to him, he picked up speed. Soon they were both running so fast that Beth had only a sense of where they were going. But she kept on following and occasionally caught glimpses of them, a flash of red hair or the swirl of Jo's dress.

"Caught him!" Jo yelled, and Beth hurried forward. Sure enough, Jo had Sean pinned to the ground. The boy was struggling, but Jo was larger and more determined. "Now we'll get your basket back," she said to Beth.

"Is that all you'd be wanting?" Sean asked. "The basket, is it?"

"You're right," Jo said to Beth. "He does talk funny."

"His words are like songs," Beth said. "And yes, I do want the basket back, Sean. It wasn't mine. It was Aunt March's."

"And I suppose that'd be the only basket such a grand lady would own," Sean said.

"She could own a hundred baskets, and that still wouldn't make the one you took yours," Jo said. She stood up and pulled Sean's arm to force him to his feet. "Now, take us to your

home so we can get Aunt March's basket and Beth won't get in trouble."

"Your kind never makes trouble for its own," Sean said. "But if you're so insistent on the basket, I suppose I could return it to you."

"That's very kind of you," Jo said.

"You don't need to be pulling at me," Sean said.

"I'm not letting you go," Jo said. "For all I know, you're one of a gang of ruffians."

"Oh, no he isn't, Jo," Beth said. "He lives with his mother. He told me."

"Joe?" Sean said. "Where's this Joe you're talking to?"

"Right here," Jo said. "Holding on to you."

"But Joe's a lad's name," Sean said. "You're a funny-looking lad."

"I won't mock your name if you don't mock mine," Jo said. "It's short for Josephine. What's Sean short for?"

"Sean Patrick O'Neill," he said. "A fine Irish name. We turn here, if you're interested, Miss Josephine."

"We are," Jo said. "We'll just take the basket and forget all about the apples. If that's all right with you, Bethy."

"It's fine," Beth said. "Aunt March really does have more apples than she knows what to do with. And actually, she told me to pick the apples for us. So it's more as if we gave the apples to Sean than that he stole them from Aunt March."

"A fine argument," Sean said. "Perhaps you be a bit Irish yourself, Miss Bethy."

"I don't think so," Beth said. "And don't call me that. Miss Bethy, I mean. There's no need for the 'Miss,' and only Jo and Marmee call me Bethy."

"And don't call me Miss Josephine either," Jo said. "Jo will do just fine."

"In Ireland such fine ladies as yourselves would demand to be called miss," Sean said, "so a lad such as me could show them the respect they're due."

"We're not in Ireland," Jo said. "And respect doesn't come from a title. It comes from the way you treat people—which includes not stealing from them."

"So it's back to that basket," Sean said. "Soon you'll be having it back, and then we'll never have need to see each other again."

"Good," Jo said. "I don't think Beth should associate with common thieves."

"Oh, no, Jo," Beth said. "Sean may be a thief, but there's really nothing common about him." To her dismay, both Jo and Sean laughed.

"You know what I mean," Beth said, feeling her face turning red.

"We're sorry," Jo said. "Aren't we, Sean?"

"Indeed I am," he said. "And I'm far more common than you might think. It's about half a mile from here. If that's too far, you can wait and I'll be getting the basket and bringing it to you."

"We're used to walking," Jo said. "Another half mile won't bother us."

They walked the remaining distance in silence. Beth thought she knew all of Concord and the area that surrounded it, but she couldn't remember ever traveling on the path they took. She could see hovels at the side of the road, shanties that looked so fragile that one good wind might blow them down. The children playing in front of them looked as frail as the shanties.

"This is my house," Sean said. "Come in, if you must."

"We must," Jo said, and she and Beth followed Sean inside.

CHAPTER 4

*I*t took Beth's eyes a moment to adjust to the darkness in Sean's home.

When Beth was finally able to see, she almost wished she had stayed outside. The only light came from the doorway; there seemed to be no windows. There wasn't much furniture, just some straw on the dirt floor and a single chair in the corner. Although it was a warm end-of-summer day, Beth shivered. She tried not to think about how cold it would get there in the fall and winter.

Beth squinted. She made out the figures of a pair of children sitting at the other end of the hovel. It was so dark, and their clothes so ragged, it was impossible to tell whether they were boys or girls.

"Why are you inside?" Sean asked them. "You should be out on such a fine day."

"Maggie has a stomachache," one of the children said.

"Kathleen says I ate too many of the apples," Maggie said. "But I was so hungry, and the apples were so good."

"Where's Mam?" Sean asked.

"Out looking for food," Kathleen said.

"Who's with you, Sean?" Maggie asked.

"Just some girls I know," Sean said. "Where's the basket, Kathleen?"

"Mam has it," the girl replied.

"She's not planning to sell it, is she?" Sean asked. "Or barter it for food?"

"No," Kathleen said. "Just to go to fields and fill it. With potatoes, she said, and cabbages, and maybe even eggs."

"She said it would be far easier to carry the food in such a fine basket," Maggie said. "And we'd have so much to eat, we wouldn't be hungry again for days. But now I feel like I'll never want to eat again."

"Mam told you not to eat so many apples," Kathleen said. "It serves you right, for you ate your share and half of mine as well. Didn't she, Sean?"

"The apples were meant for all of us," Sean said. "Maggie was just faster getting to them."

"But what about the basket?" Jo asked. "Beth needs it back."

Sean turned to Beth. "I'm sorry," he said. "Me mam might be gone for hours. It's not as if the fine people of Concord leave their food just waiting for the likes of her to find."

"That's all right," Beth said. "Let her take her time. We can always get the basket some other day."

"But Beth," Jo said, "if we leave the basket with them, you'll never get it back."

"We don't know that," Beth said. "Sean, we'll come back in a day or two to get the basket. Is that all right with you?"

"It's fine with me," he said very softly. "I'll be thanking you for that courtesy."

"Come, Jo," Beth said. "We still have to get the flour for Hannah."

"I'll be walking you back," Sean said. "Fine ladies like you shouldn't walk this path alone."

"We'll be all right," Beth said. "Thank you anyway, Sean."

"I don't like any of this," Jo muttered, but she followed Beth outside. "You know that basket is gone for good, don't you? You're going to have to tell Aunt March."

"I'm not going to tell her anything," Beth said as they walked back toward town. "Jo, didn't you see how they were living? Those poor children, the way they talked about being hungry . . . You should have seen how Sean devoured that apple yesterday. Now I know why. What difference does it make to Aunt March if she loses a basket? They were starving, Jo."

Jo looked at Beth. "Aunt March won't see it that way," she said. "And I'm afraid she'll hold you responsible, when it wasn't your fault."

"I'll have to take that chance," said Beth. She pictured Aunt March as a hungry tiger, then made herself think of other things. "What can we do for them?" she asked. "The O'Neills, I mean."

"I know who you mean," Jo said. "Isn't the basket enough?"

"Oh, Jo," Beth said. "I know you're upset for my sake, but we simply have to help those people. It isn't right that they should starve when we have so much."

"We don't have that much," Jo said. "True, we don't go hungry or wear rags, but we're not rich either, Bethy, and don't get it into your head that we are."

"Aunt March is," Beth said.

"But Aunt March isn't helping them," Jo replied. "And knowing Aunt March, she never would."

"Then we'll have to," Beth said. "Do you think if I gave them my fifty cents, they could use it?"

"Beth, you need that money to replace the basket," Jo said.

"But Sean will return the basket," Beth said. "And then I won't need the fifty cents. I know it isn't much, Jo, but I don't know what else I have to give them."

Jo was silent for what felt to Beth like a long time. "If Sean actually gives you back the basket, I'll give you my twenty five cents," she said finally.

"Oh, Jo, thank you!" Beth said. "How much food do you think seventy-five cents could buy?"

"Not enough," Jo said. "But maybe we could get Meg to give us some money as well."

"And Amy too," Beth said.

Jo laughed. "You'll stand a better chance with Aunt March," she said. "But maybe Amy will give up some of her old clothes for Kathleen and Maggie."

"Jo, can you imagine what it must be like to live that way?" Beth asked. "No food. No beds. No shoes."

"No," Jo said. "I really can't."

Beth was startled. Jo had a wonderful imagination. She was always writing plays for her sisters to perform, all about dukes and princesses and terrible curses. It had never occurred to Beth that there might be something Jo couldn't imagine.

"I don't think it's right that people should have to live that way," Beth said. "I know we don't have much, but we have all we need and enough left over for ribbons at Christmas. And Aunt March must have twenty apple trees all for herself."

"And her servants," Jo said. "And she gives us food from her gardens as well."

"It still isn't right," Beth said. "When I grow up, Jo, I'm going to devote my life to helping the poor. If you think there will still be poor people then."

"I'm afraid there always will be," Jo said. "You help as many as you can, Bethy. Just as many as you can."

CHAPTER 5

" *I* don't understand," Amy said. "I'm supposed to give away my clothes to some ragamuffins I've never met because one of them stole a basket from Beth?"

"It sounds to me as though you understand perfectly," Jo said. "Be an angel, Amy, and give up something. It will make Beth feel so much better."

"This isn't about me," Beth said. "It's for those poor children. Amy, they have nothing. No dolls, no toys, no books."

"No clothes either, it sounds like," Meg said. The four sisters were sitting in Beth and

Amy's bedroom. Beth had never noticed how much she owned before. She looked at her doll collection. It wasn't much, she knew. She had a fondness for dolls that needed love, and so many of her dolls were missing an arm or a leg or even a head. But she loved each and every one of them and didn't know what her life would be like without them.

"They were in wretched shape," Jo said. "The children, I mean. We could hardly see their clothes, it was so dark in there."

"If you couldn't see their clothes, maybe they were fine," said Amy. "Maybe they were very well dressed."

"Oh, no," Jo said. "We saw what Sean was wearing. They were in rags, all right."

"I don't see why I should be the one to have to sacrifice," Amy said. "I always get the worst clothes anyway. The three of you have worn things till they're hardly more than patches. Why doesn't Meg give up one of her dresses?"

"Amy, you hold on to everything," Jo said. "We're not asking you to give up anything you're using now. Just some of the older things that you wear when you're painting or making some other kind of mess of yourself."

"I never make a mess of myself, Jo March!" said Amy. "And I need those clothes for painting in. I'm not like you, willing to get ink stains all over my prettiest dresses. Besides, what are those Irish people doing in Concord anyway? If they liked it so much in Ireland, why did they ever leave?"

"There was a terrible famine in Ireland a few years ago," Meg said. "People starved to death. A lot of the Irish came to America then to try to make better lives for themselves."

"But if the famine stopped, why didn't they stay in Ireland or go back there?" Amy asked.

"I don't think things are much better there now," Meg said. "Perhaps the O'Neills thought they and their children would find a better life in America."

"Things must have been pretty bad in Ireland for it to seem better here," said Jo. "Meg, you can't imagine how desperate they are."

"I have a little money saved up," Meg said.

"I was hoping to buy a new pair of gloves, but it sounds as though the O'Neills need the money more than I need the gloves."

"And I'm going to give them one of my dolls," said Beth. "No, two of them, one for Maggie and one for Kathleen. And my fifty cents, and I'm sure I can find some clothes I no longer need."

"And what will you give them, Jo?" asked Amy.

"All my money, which isn't very much," Jo replied. "And I'll go through my things as well. I must have something they can use that we don't need here."

"Amy, we know you have something you can give them," Meg said. "And think how good you'll feel when you do."

Meg had a way of getting Amy to do things that none of the others, not even Marmee, had. "I was saving money for new paintbrushes," Amy said. "I suppose I can get by with my old ones a little while longer."

Beth gave Amy a big hug. "Now I'll see what food Hannah can spare," she said. "Once

37

we gather everything together, I'll give it to Sean for his family."

"I'll go with you," said Jo. "You shouldn't be walking around there by yourself, Beth. Besides, you'll have too much to carry on your own."

The girls went downstairs. Hannah was nowhere to be seen. "I think I'll just take some food," said Beth. "You go upstairs and get all our things together. I want Maggie to have Esmeralda and Kathleen to have Caroline. You know which ones they are, don't you, Jo?"

"Of course I do," Jo said. "But are you sure you want to give them away? They're both very nice dolls."

"They need me less than my other dolls do," Beth said. "And I can't give those girls dolls that are missing arms and legs. Just pack them with the other things, and I'll meet you at the front door."

Jo nodded and left Beth in the kitchen. Beth felt funny about taking things without permission, but she was so sure Marmee and

Father would approve that she saw no reason to worry. Instead she put potatoes, bread, beans, and preserves in a bag. She wished she could take eggs, but she was afraid they'd break.

"I'm glad Marmee is out with Father," Jo said as the girls began their journey. "We'd have a lot of explaining to do."

"But surely they'd approve," Beth said. "They're always telling us to think of others and what we can do to help them."

"True," Jo said. "But I don't think they included raiding the larder. Did you leave any food for us to eat?"

"We won't go hungry," Beth said.

"Amy gave up a pair of shoes," Jo said. "Of course they no longer fit her, so there was no need for her to keep them. But even so it was hard for her to part with them. Meg and I told her she was quite a saint, and she seemed to agree!"

"Amy has a good heart," said Beth. "She just doesn't always remember to show it."

The girls talked some more, then walked silently. It was a long journey to the O'Neills', and more than once Beth regretted having so much to carry in food and so little in money.

"I think I see Sean," Jo said as they neared his home. "He'll be surprised to see us again so soon and with so much for his family. Sean! Sean!"

It was indeed Sean, and he walked over to them. "What's this?" he asked.

"Just some things for you and your sisters," Beth said. "Some food and clothes."

"And two of Bethy's dolls," Jo said. "She loves those dolls so, you should feel quite honored. They're for your sisters, of course."

"And my sisters and I are giving you all our money," said Beth. "It isn't very much, we know, but we want to help as much as we can."

"And who asked for your help?" asked Sean. "We're not charity cases, you know. We'd work if we could, we're none of us afraid of it."

"Don't you speak to Beth that way," said Jo.

41

"It's all right," Beth said.

"No, it isn't," Jo said. "This has nothing to do with whether you're willing to work, Sean O'Neill. It has to do with what you need right now. And that's food and clothes and money. And dolls. You may not need dolls, but your sisters will be happier for having them."

"How is Maggie?" Beth asked. "Is she feeling any better?"

"And did your mother come back with the basket?" Jo asked.

"You'll be getting your precious basket back soon enough," said Sean. "And yes, Maggie is much improved, thank you."

"Good," Beth said. "Jo, let's just leave all this with Sean. He'll do with it what he wants. We have a long walk home."

CHAPTER 6

*A*s Beth and Jo walked back home, they ran into Gertrude Eberley and Charles Gordon, two children who were in the same class as Beth. Beth didn't particularly like either of them, but she nonetheless said hello.

"Did I see you running toward Shantytown earlier?" Charles asked Jo.

"Shantytown?" Jo asked. "Where's that?"

"That's where the Irish live," Gertrude replied. "No decent people go there."

"And why not?" Jo asked. Beth was glad Jo was with her, since she never knew what to say to the likes of Charles and Gertrude.

"The Irish aren't like us," Gertrude replied. "Everyone knows that. They're dirty and illiterate. And Papa says they're idol worshippers."

"They're not fit to be in this country," Charles declared. "That's what my father says. He believes it's a crime that they've come over and that they should all go back to Ireland before they become a real nuisance."

"I haven't noticed any of them bothering me," Jo said. "Or you either, for that matter, Charles."

"Are you calling my father a liar?" Charles asked. "If you are, I'd punch you good if you weren't a girl."

"Punch me anyway, I dare you," Jo said, looking more than willing to fight Charles.

"Stop it!" Beth yelled, hardly believing she had the courage to speak. "I have a friend who's Irish and he's a fine person. Smart and strong. It's not his fault he's poor."

"Are you saying it's our fault?" Gertrude asked. "No one I know told them to come over and build those dreadful shanties in our town."

"I don't know whose fault it is," Beth said. "But it isn't my friend's. And it doesn't help when people like you say nasty things. I'll bet you've never even met an Irish person."

"I have," Charles said. "My mother hired one to help with the washing."

"My mother refuses to hire them," Gertrude said. "She says all the Irish are unreliable."

"And all people named Eberley are terrible snobs," Beth said.

"Bethy!" Jo said, but Beth could see that she was amused.

"All I mean is, nobody's exactly like anybody else," Beth said. "How can all the Irish be exactly the same, any more than all the Eberleys or all the Marches? I'm nothing like you, Jo, and you're nothing like Meg or Amy. So if *we're* not alike, then the Irish can't all be alike either."

"I don't know what your point is," Gertrude said. "But I think you've insulted my family, and that's very wrong of you."

"And what makes it all right for you to insult all the Irish?" Beth asked.

Gertrude huffed. "Decent people wouldn't live in Shantytown," she declared. "Even the Marches wouldn't choose to live that way."

"Why, thank you, Gertrude," Jo said. "That's probably the nicest thing you've ever said about my family."

Charles laughed. "She has you there, Gertrude," he said. "Besides, everyone knows how the Marches are. They're always fighting for the poor and the unfortunate."

"What's wrong with that?" Jo asked.

"It won't make you rich," said Charles.

"There are more important things than being rich," said Beth. "Like helping those in need."

"My family helps the poor and the unfortunate too," Gertrude said. "But they should be worthy of our help. And you may be right, Beth. Maybe there are some Irish who are decent folk, but my parents have yet to meet any."

"My father says the Irish want to live the way they do," Charles announced. "He says that's how they lived back in Ireland, sharing their huts with pigs and chickens. He says they don't believe in cleanliness."

"Then why has your mother hired one to do the washing?" Jo asked.

"Because my mother was taking pity on the poor unfortunates," Charles said. "I believe it was your mother who talked her into it."

"That sounds like Mrs. March," Gertrude said. Jo glowered at her. "Worrying about the poor, I mean."

"I saw a sign once," Charles said. "At a hotel. It said 'No dogs or Irish.'" He laughed.

"What an awful thing to say," Beth said. "How would you feel if you saw a sign like that about your people?"

"But there never would be such a sign," Charles replied. "My people, as you call them, are respectable members of society. As long as the Irish aren't, they will be treated differently. That's just the way of the world."

"Then there's something wrong with the world," Beth said, and she ran away from Charles and Gertrude and their wicked, bigoted words.

"Bethy, wait up," Jo said, rushing to catch up with her sister.

Beth slowed down.

"My, you are in a mood," Jo said. "I can't ever remember having to ask you to wait for me. It's always the other way around."

"I hated what they were saying," Beth declared.

"And you certainly told them so," said Jo. "Father would have been proud of you. You're so shy, Beth, but when you care deeply about something, you fight for it, just the same as he does."

"No one should have to live the way Sean's family does," Beth said. "And then for people to say that's how the Irish want to live . . ." She became enraged all over again.

"I know you're right, Bethy," Jo said. "But people do say terrible things about each other. Think of what Aunt March says about us."

"Now you're making jokes!" Beth cried. "I would have thought you at least would feel for those poor people. You saw how they live, Jo, how terrible things are for them."

"Oh, Beth," Jo said. "You're much kinder than I'll ever be. You're like Marmee that way, caring about others even if you don't know them. I care about us, but about me most of all. I don't have a good heart, the way you do."

"You have the best heart of anybody I know," Beth said. "And the smartest brain. Now tell me what we're going to do to help Sean and his family."

"You mean more than we've already done?" Jo asked. "I'm not sure there is anything we can do, Beth."

But Beth refused to believe it. If Jo couldn't figure out a way, perhaps Father could.

CHAPTER 7

Beth waited until after supper to talk with Father. He was sitting in his chair by the window, reading a newspaper by the late summer sun.

"What is it, child?" he asked Beth as she sat by his feet.

"Father, are we poor?" she asked him.

"Not in the ways that matter," he said. "We have each other and our health and this home to call our own. What more could we wish for?"

"I could wish for a great deal," Amy said from her corner of the room.

"But what would you sacrifice to get it?"

50

Father asked. "Would you give up one of your sisters for a diamond necklace, Amy? Is your health worth an emerald ring?"

"Don't push her, Father," Jo said with a laugh. "She might decide I am worth a diamond or two."

"As though I could get a diamond for you," Amy retorted. All the girls laughed.

"Very well," Father said. "We won't trade any of us for jewelry."

"Oh, dear," Marmee said. "And I was just offered the loveliest tiara for you, dearest."

The whole family laughed then. "You're the jewel in my crown," Father said to Marmee. "When I look at you, I believe myself to be the richest man in the world."

"But do we have a lot of money?" Beth asked.

Father laughed. "Of all my daughters, you're the last one I would have thought would ever ask me that," he said. "What's come over you, Beth, that you're suddenly so interested in riches?"

"I thought perhaps if we had money, we

51

might be able to help the less fortunate," Beth said. "There are so many needy people."

"You have a generous heart," Father replied. "But I'm afraid there are far too many for us to help them all."

"But could we help a family?" Beth asked. "Just one family?"

"We try to help many families," Father said. "We've all done without things that bring us pleasure so that some child might have food to eat or a blanket to keep warm with."

"I know I've made my share of sacrifices," Meg said. "We all have, Beth, quite recently, in fact."

"But it's not fair," Beth said. "Why should some people like Gertrude Eberley have so much, and others have so very little?"

"Gertrude Eberley?" Amy asked. "She doesn't have so very much. She has more than we have, I suppose, but she isn't truly rich. I know. I've been to her home."

"The Howes have more money than the Eberleys," Meg said. "Quite a few families in Concord have more than the Eberleys."

"I'm not sure I like my little women to be able to judge so accurately who has money and who hasn't," Father said. "Surely Gertrude Eberley should be judged on some other basis than her family's wealth."

"But she judges others on how poor they are," Beth said.

"Did Gertrude Eberley say something mean about us?" Amy asked. "I hate it when people look down on us because we don't have money."

"Gertrude didn't say anything mean about us," Jo said. "But Beth and I ran into her today and she said terrible things about the Irish. Charles Gordon did also."

Father shook his head. "Many people have prejudices against the Irish," he said. "Their religion and customs are different from ours, and that always disturbs people."

"But they don't deserve to be poor," Beth said. "Really poor, I mean. At least we own a home and have Hannah to help us, and we never go hungry. But it breaks my heart to think of how little the Irish have."

"We cannot help all the poor," Marmee said, "much as we might like to. No one is rich enough to do that."

"Not even Aunt March?" Beth asked.

"Not even she," Marmee said.

"Even if she were rich enough, she wouldn't," Jo grumbled. "Aunt March believes only in charity for herself."

"That's not fair and not true," Marmee said. "She's been very kind to many families over the years, including our own."

"And she would give us more if we would accept it," Father said. "It's hard to achieve a balance when it comes to giving and receiving. Beth, I believe, would give away the clothes on her back to help someone in need. She feels that way because her heart is loving and giving. But there are others—and I'm not saying Aunt March is one of them—who give so that they can feel a sense of superiority over others. Or they give so that they can control others."

"How can that be?" Amy asked.

"A father might give his son a house," Father replied, "so that the son will live nearby, or so that the son will make a room for his father to live in."

"Or a father might send his son to Europe," Marmee said, "to break up a love affair the son is having with a woman the father finds unsuitable. Those are gifts that control."

"Does Aunt March offer us those sorts of gifts?" Meg asked.

"Not exactly," Father said. "But she has strong opinions about the way we should live, and I suspect that if we accepted more of her charity, she'd feel she had a stronger right to offer her opinions."

"A stronger right!" cried Jo. "As though she keeps those opinions to herself now!"

"When I'm rich, I shall be very good and kind," declared Amy. "Not as good and kind as Beth might be, but good and kind nonetheless. I shall be known for it, as well as for my beauty and my great artistic ability. And my lovely home." She was silent for a moment. "And my jewelry and clothes."

Her sisters burst out laughing. "That's quite a lot to be known for," Meg said. "With all that, you'll be the best-known woman in America."

"And what's wrong with that?" Amy asked.

"Nothing," Marmee said. "As long as you're known for the right reasons. Kindness. Artistic talent. Even a beautiful home, if it's filled with love. Those are things to be proud of."

"I'll be famous for being a great writer," Jo said. "And I'll make lots and lots of money from it, and give it all to you, Bethy, for you to help the poor."

"I'll give you money also, Beth," Amy said. "Between Jo and me, you'll be so rich you'll be famous too!"

Beth joined her sisters in laughter. But she couldn't help thinking of Sean and his family and wondering whether they would see the humor the way the Marches could.

CHAPTER 8

*B*eth had a hard time falling asleep that night. She kept thinking about how Sean lived and what it must be like to go to bed hungry. Not that he even had a bed to go to. She pictured his sisters playing with Esmeralda and Caroline, but her image of Maggie and Kathleen was so sorrowful, she had difficulty picturing them enjoying themselves.

I should have brought them more food, she thought. Food was what they needed, and clothing. They'd freeze to death in the winter if they didn't get some warmer clothes to wear, as well as shoes. If she'd only had more money to give them! But she and Jo and Meg and Amy had less than two dollars among them, and while that would certainly help the O'Neills, it wouldn't mean the difference between survival and starvation in the winter, when there would be no food for them to take from other people's gardens.

It's so unfair, Beth thought. Her family had an apple tree and they picked its apples and ate them through the winter months. Aunt March had at least twenty apple trees, and most of her apples just rotted away. The O'Neills had nothing; Aunt March had food that was never used.

Beth listened to Amy's deep breathing. She told herself to fall asleep, but it was no use. Instead she let her mind wander through Aunt March's house with all its beautiful possessions. True, she and Jo, Meg, and Amy had little money to give to the O'Neills. But Aunt March had a house filled with objects worth hundreds of dollars each. She owned so much that she couldn't possibly enjoy what she had.

And the O'Neills had so little, they could die from want.

Abandoning all thoughts of sleep, Beth sat up in her bed. She and her sisters had given up all they could. She didn't dare take any more food from their larder. Hannah complained enough how hard it was to feed them all on what little they had. But Aunt March . . . Aunt March owned the world, or at least most of it. She owned enough to keep the O'Neills from starving.

Beth's first thought was to take food from Aunt March. But that wouldn't work, she decided. There were always servants in the kitchen, and they would notice if Beth was there for no reason. Besides, she'd have to carry an awful lot of food for the O'Neills to have enough when the cold weather hit. No, it would have to be money, or something the O'Neills could turn into money.

Again Beth pictured Aunt March's house. It was filled with silver. People sold their silver in times of need; she'd heard Marmee and Father discuss people's doing that. All she would have to do was take one little silver thing, a tray or a candlestick or a bowl, and give it to the O'Neills. Sean's mother could sell it, and then the family would have enough money to last them quite a while.

It was such a wonderful idea that Beth thought about waking up Jo to discuss it with her. But Jo was still angry about the basket. Beth didn't think Jo would care to hear any more about helping out the O'Neills.

And Beth knew she couldn't discuss it with Marmee or Father either. They might agree with her that Aunt March owned far too many things and the O'Neills far too few, but she couldn't see them agreeing with Beth that the best solution was to take something from Aunt March and give it to the O'Neills.

Nor, Beth knew, would Aunt March approve. There was no point in asking her when the answer would be no. Beth would have to do it on her own.

That's stealing, she told herself, and stealing is wrong. She'd told Sean it was a sin just the other day. And it was still a sin.

But letting children starve was a greater one, she reasoned. A silver tray was nothing to Aunt March and the world to the O'Neills.

It shouldn't be that hard. All Beth would have to do was go over to Aunt March's in the morning. Aunt March always paid her calls on Wednesday mornings, so she wouldn't even be home. Williams would let Beth in, and Beth could make up a reason for being there. She could say she had lost one of her dolls and thought perhaps she'd left it at Aunt March's. Williams would leave her alone while she searched, and she'd find something silver that Aunt March would be unlikely to miss and slip it under her dress. Then she'd tell Williams, if she saw him again, that she'd found her doll, and she'd leave. She'd go straight to the O'Neills and give Sean what she'd taken. He couldn't claim it was charity, because charity came from what you owned, not what you stole from somebody else.

Nobody ever turned down Robin Hood, Beth said to herself. And he was a hero, robbing from the rich and giving to the poor. That was all she'd be doing. If she took from Aunt March to have nice things for herself, that would be a sin and she would deserve to be punished. But as long as she was doing it to help others, it was all right. She was sure even Father would agree to that, although she thought it best not to ask him.

Beth lay down on her bed and closed her eyes. There were so many different things she could take. It had to be something small and easy to carry but still worth lots and lots of money.

Something small, she thought just before she fell asleep. Something small. She dreamed that she was something small and Aunt March was a giant tiger. Beth was so tiny that Aunt March the tiger stepped right over her and never even noticed she was there.

eth woke up the next morning even more excited about her plan. It was so simple, really, and it would mean so much to the O'Neills. But she knew better than to show everybody how she felt. It would be hardest to keep it a secret from Jo, so Beth decided to have as little to do with her that morning as possible.

"I'm missing some food," Hannah said to Marmee at breakfast. "There's a loaf of bread gone, and some preserves, and I don't know what else."

"Are you sure you haven't just miscounted?"

Marmee asked. "We do go through a lot of food daily, Hannah."

"Don't I know it," Hannah said as Beth and her sisters exchanged guilty glances. "And I keep a watchful eye on what's there for just that reason. This food is missing."

Beth waited for her mother to ask the girls if they knew what had happened, but apparently it didn't cross Marmee's mind that they might. "Make do with what you have, Hannah," Marmee said. "I'll speak to Mr. March this evening and see if he gave it to one of his poor parishioners. They might have needed it more than we do."

"There's such a thing as too much charity," Hannah grumbled as she left the room.

"There certainly is," Amy whispered, and her sisters all burst out laughing.

"What do you find so funny?" Marmee asked, smiling.

"Nothing, Marmee," said Meg. "Just Amy's attitudes about charity."

"I only think it begins at home," said Amy.

"It's true we should take care of ourselves,"

Marmee said. "But our hearts must always be open to those in greater need than ourselves. Your father and I believe that deeply, and we hope our daughters believe it as well."

"We do, Marmee," Jo said. "Including Amy."

Marmee smiled again at her daughters. "Then perhaps you'll go with me as I make my rounds of the parishioners," she said. "It would brighten their spirits to see you girls. Amy, you're a particular pet of so many of them. Could you spare them your morning to cheer them up?"

"Must I be the only one to go with you?" Amy asked. "How about Beth? She never goes."

"Oh, no," Beth said. "I can't."

"You know how shy Beth is," Jo said. "It would be torture for her to have to make calls."

"Then you could go in her place," said Amy.

"No, I can't," Jo said. "I promised Father I'd help him set up for the meeting he has tonight. I'll be busy all morning moving tables and chairs around. Unless you'd prefer to do that, Amy."

"I'll go with you also, Marmee," said Meg. "It can be tedious, and it's unfair to ask Amy to shoulder the burden alone."

"You're all good girls," said Marmee. "Beth, will you find something that will occupy you this morning?"

"Oh, yes," Beth said. "I'll find something to do."

"Very well," Marmee said. "After breakfast, we'll do our chores and then take care of our obligations."

Beth tried to act as normal as possible while she and her sisters completed their chores. But she felt a great sense of relief as first Jo, then Marmee, Meg, and Amy left the house. She'd never thought going to Aunt March's would feel easier than staying home, but this morning it certainly did.

It was a cloudy day, and a few raindrops were already falling when Beth reached Aunt March's. She knocked at the door, and Williams opened it.

"Hello," Beth said, willing herself to sound as normal as possible. "Is my aunt in?"

"I'm afraid not, Miss Beth," Williams said. "She's out paying her calls."

"Oh, that's right," Beth said, feeling almost exhilarated at being able to play her part so well. "It's Wednesday, and she's always out on Wednesdays."

"Perhaps there's something I can do to help," Williams said.

"It's just that I can't find one of my dolls," Beth said. "Annabelle. And she's a favorite of mine. I thought perhaps I left her here when I was visiting the other day."

"Mrs. March has not mentioned finding Annabelle," said Williams.

"She's small," Beth said. "Annabelle, that is." And in spite of herself, she giggled nervously.

But Williams only smiled. "Would you like me to look for her?" he asked. "Annabelle, that is?"

"No, I will," Beth said. "I'm sure Aunt March wouldn't mind."

"Very well, miss," said Williams. "Please let me know if you find her. Otherwise I'll have the servants look through the house for her."

"Thank you," Beth said. Williams let her into the house, and Beth cast a look around the front hallway. There were things there worth taking, but their absence would be easily noticed. She'd do better in one of the parlors, or perhaps the dining room.

The parlors would be easier, she decided, because there was no reason for Annabelle to be in the dining room. And while the front parlor had more things in it, she'd really only been in the back parlor. So if there was anyone in the front parlor, she'd excuse herself and hope the back parlor was empty.

But none of the servants was in the front parlor. Beth breathed a sigh of relief as she looked in the room. Then she grew excited. It was filled with so many things, Aunt March would certainly never notice if one of them was missing.

Beth looked at the candlesticks. They were

worth a great deal, she was sure, but she couldn't take one without the other, and Aunt March probably used them at night. So they wouldn't do. There was a lovely silver tray on a corner table, but when Beth tried slipping it under her dress, it proved far too bulky.

Then Beth spotted the perfect thing. It was a small silver bowl, tucked away on a little table in a dark corner of the room. She couldn't imagine Aunt March spending any time at all in that corner, and it would probably be years before she noticed the bowl was gone, and by then she'd have no idea where it could have gotten to.

Beth picked the bowl up and examined it carefully. It was small but very beautiful, and she was sure it had great value. Perhaps one day she'd be able to buy it back for Aunt March, but in the meantime, she was sure it would keep the O'Neills from starving.

The next problem was how to carry it out of the house. There'd be no trouble if Beth could be sure none of the servants would see her.

But if any of them did, they would certainly ask why she was taking the bowl. She needed to hide it.

It had all seemed so easy the night before. Beth had pictured a tray somehow balancing itself under her skirt as she glided out of Aunt March's house. But the bowl didn't seem willing to balance itself. Twice it slipped out from under her skirt as she attempted to leave the room. Both times she was able to catch it right before it crashed to the floor.

She tried then to slip it through the neck of her dress, but the dress was too tight. She unbuttoned the front and put the bowl on her chest, but then the dress wouldn't button up. She thought about wearing the bowl on her head, as though it were a bonnet, but then she started shaking with silent laughter. She forced herself to calm down. She didn't have forever, and she and the bowl had to get out of there soon.

She lifted her skirt and looked down at her pantaloons. Perhaps she could put the bowl inside them. The bowl would certainly slip

down, but not, if Beth was lucky, until she was outside. Then she could get the bowl out and carry it to the O'Neills.

The pantaloons would have to be the solution, she decided. She began to put the bowl inside them when a noise made her turn around.

"Beth March! Whatever are you doing!"

CHAPTER 10

eth nearly dropped the bowl. "Aunt March," she said. "I thought you were out."

"I was," Aunt March replied. "But it was raining and I decided to make my calls some other day. What are you doing with that bowl?"

Before Beth had a chance to answer, Williams appeared at the parlor door, dragging Sean behind him. "This lad appeared here just now with a basket he says belongs to you, Mrs. March," Williams said.

"And who might you be?" Aunt March asked.

"Sean O'Neill," Sean said. "Begging your pardon, ma'am, but would you mind asking this man of yours to stop pulling at my ear?"

"Williams," Aunt March said, and the butler promptly released Sean.

"Sean," Beth said. "Why did you come here?"

"You two know each other?" Aunt March asked.

Sean ignored her. "It was your aunt's basket I took, so it's back to her I brought it," he replied.

"I knew you would," Beth said. "Wait until I tell Jo."

"I still want to know what you're doing with that bowl," Aunt March said. "It appeared to me you were slipping it inside certain private garments, Beth."

"Beth," Sean said, "was this another one of your charitable ideas?"

"No," Beth said. "I mean, I suppose you might think so, but I didn't."

"I think perhaps she was taking it for me,"

Sean said. "And my family. Beth has it in her head that we could use a bit of help."

"Well, you can," Beth said. "Aunt March, they live in the most dreadful poverty. And you have so many things, I didn't think you'd miss just one."

"That one I would have missed," Aunt March said. "It's a Paul Revere bowl that my father gave me as a wedding gift."

"Oh," Beth said. "If I had known that, I would have taken something else. But I still would have taken something, because the O'Neills will starve if we don't help them."

"I find it hard to believe this is you speaking," Aunt March said. "I don't think you've ever said more than five words to me, and those only when your mother forced you to."

"I'm sorry, Aunt March," Beth said. "About talking so much, I mean."

"You should be sorry about stealing," Aunt March said.

"That would be my fault," Sean said. "She was doing it for me. Not that I asked her to."

"No, he didn't," Beth said. "Honestly, Aunt March. Nobody knew anything about it. It was all my idea."

Aunt March stared at the children. "Stealing is wrong," she said. "Whether you steal from me or from anyone else, Beth."

"Starving's wrong too," Beth said.

"I'm sure you're exaggerating this family's condition," Aunt March said. "Many families have hard times. Your own has had its share. But you've never come close to starving."

"Sean, tell her," Beth said.

"We'll do fine," Sean said instead. "Without the help of thievery."

"Aunt March, you have to see how they live," Beth said. "Please. Just meet them once, and then if you think I'm exaggerating, I'll take any punishment you think just. I'll even go to jail. But you have to see them first."

"Marches do not go to jail," Aunt March declared. "But I have nothing else to do this morning, so I might as well see what has you so upset that you're actually speaking. Williams, call for my carriage. We are going to take a ride."

"Yes, ma'am," Williams said. A few moments later he returned to announce that the carriage awaited them.

Even for Beth, riding in Aunt March's carriage was a thrill. She could hardly guess how Sean must feel, getting into such a beautiful vehicle, one that took two horses to pull.

But Sean kept quiet, and so did Beth and Aunt March. Sean directed the driver, and as they got closer to where he lived, Beth noticed that people were coming out of their shanties and staring at the carriage.

"I didn't know these huts existed," Aunt March said. "It's a disgrace."

Sean told the driver to stop in front of his home. Aunt March got out gingerly, as though she were afraid the mud from the rain would damage her.

"That's my mam," Sean said as a tired-looking woman came out of the hut. "And my sisters, Maggie and Kathleen. Mam, this is

Beth, the one I've told you so much about. And this grand lady is her aunt March."

Mrs. O'Neill curtsied. "It's an honor to be meeting you," she said.

"May I come in?" Aunt March asked.

"Certainly," Mrs. O'Neill said. "Girls, make room for Mrs. March."

Maggie and Kathleen scurried out of the way. Aunt March walked in through the makeshift door.

"This is terrible," Aunt March said. "No one should be living like this in Concord."

"We're sorry, ma'am," Mrs. O'Neill said. "We keep it as clean as possible, but it's terribly hard."

"It's raining inside," Aunt March said.

"It always does," Kathleen said. "There was a fierce storm last week, and we thought we'd drown, it rained so hard inside."

"Shush," Mrs. O'Neill said. "Mrs. March doesn't need to hear about such things."

"Yes, I do," Aunt March said. "How long have you been living like this?"

"Since last spring," Sean said. "We were in

Boston before then, but the streets were so bad, we feared for the girls. And we thought perhaps we could find work here."

"Your clothes," Aunt March said. "Do you have better than what you're wearing?"

"No, ma'am," Kathleen said. "What we own is on our backs."

"We have enough," Sean said.

"Stop it," Beth said. "You don't. You wear rags and you don't own any shoes and if it weren't for the apples you took, you and your sisters would have starved."

"Times have been hard," Mrs. O'Neill said. "But if I could only find work, I'd be taking better care of my children and seeing they don't go hungry."

"Tell me, Mrs. O'Neill, do you know how to clean houses?" Aunt March asked.

"That I do," Mrs. O'Neill said. "I can scrub and sweep and polish."

"I need a new housemaid," Aunt March said. "And my gardener could use an apprentice if this young man would be willing."

"I would be most willing," said Sean.

"If the two of you will work for me, your family can move into a small cottage I have on my estate," Aunt March said. "Would that be acceptable to you, Mrs. O'Neill?"

"Yes, my lady," Mrs. O'Neill said. "You're sent from Heaven, you are."

"I'm not your lady," Aunt March said. "This is America, and if you are to live here, you must start thinking as Americans do. But if Heaven sent me to help you, then we should all be grateful to the Good Lord, because I for one have great need of a new housemaid, and my gardener could use a hardworking apprentice."

"Thank you, Beth," Sean said. "It was work that we wanted, not charity, and thanks to you, we have it."

"I'll see you soon," Beth said. "At Aunt March's. You can pick some apples for me."

"Come, Beth," Aunt March said. "I need to pay some calls after all—on the good people of Concord to ask them what they intend to do about conditions here."

"Yes, Aunt March," Beth said. She followed

her great-aunt to the carriage. They kept quiet until they were close to town, and then Beth knew she had to speak.

"Aunt March," she said, "I'm ready to take my punishment. What shall we do about the bowl I tried to take?"

"It's a good thing for you that it was a Paul Revere bowl," Aunt March said. "It shows you possess a keen eye for what is valuable. Besides, he was a revolutionary, and I can see we need to shake things up here once again!"

Beth couldn't help it. She laughed. And much to her surprise and delight, Aunt March laughed right along with her.

CHAPTER 11

*I*t was the first day of school. But instead of walking with Amy as she usually did, Beth found herself standing in Aunt March's front parlor. In spite of herself, she took a quick look at the Paul Revere bowl. She was glad it was still in its proper place.

"Beth," said Aunt March, walking into the room. "Thank you for coming here so early."

Beth was unaccustomed to Aunt March's thanking her for anything and didn't know what to say.

"I've asked you here because I need a favor from you," Aunt March continued, and now

Beth was truly confused. "It concerns the O'Neill children."

"What about them?" Beth asked. "They're all right, aren't they?"

"They certainly are," Aunt March said. "Now that they have some food in them and a roof over their heads and decent clothes and shoes."

"I'm so glad," Beth said. "You've been very kind to them, Aunt March."

"Their mother is a good worker," Aunt March replied. "And Sean isn't afraid of getting his hands dirty. The girls are pleasant enough, and I'm sure one day they'll be fine workers too."

"Then what favor do you need from me?" Beth asked.

"The children are going to school today," Aunt March said. "I thought you might be willing to show them the way."

"School?" Beth asked.

"You sound surprised," Aunt March said. "Do you think I gave them work and a home so that they could become ignorant little hooligans?"

"No, Aunt March," Beth said.

"They need an education," Aunt March said. "How else can they be good Americans? Their mother and I agreed about that. Of course she'd rather they went to a church school, but since one isn't available, the school in town will have to do. It's been good enough for four generations of Marches, after all. Now they're waiting outside for you. And, Beth . . ."

"Yes, Aunt March?"

"I think they're a little nervous," Aunt March said softly. "That's why I've asked you to go with them."

"Of course I will, Aunt March," Beth said. She went to her aunt and kissed her on the cheek. "You're a good woman, Aunt March," she said.

"I don't need you to tell me that," Aunt March harrumphed, but even that didn't frighten Beth. She left Aunt March's house and found Sean, Maggie, and Kathleen standing outside.

"So you're going to school with me," she said to them.

"Of course we are," Sean said. "It's a good education we'll be needing if we're not to be common laborers all our lives."

"Sean wants to be a doctor someday," Kathleen said. "And help the poor and sickly ones."

"I think he'll be a wonderful doctor," Beth said.

"If I become one, it'll be thanks to you," said Sean. "And that fine aunt of yours. What a grand lady she turned out to be. She demands a day's work for a day's wages, but there's no pity in her kindness."

"Mam says Mrs. March always treats her with respect," said Maggie. "Mam says she's never been treated that way before, not in all the years she lived in Ireland."

"That's because this is America," Beth said. "Where we're all equals. Or we will be when the slaves are freed and women get the vote."

"There's such a lot to work for," said Kathleen. "But with food in my stomach, I do believe I can do it all."

Beth's laughter was choked off by the sight of Charles Gordon and Gertrude Eberley walking toward the school.

"What's making you so nervous, Beth?" Sean asked.

"Nothing," Beth said. "Just ignore that boy and girl up ahead."

"I'll be ignoring no one," said Sean, and he walked right over to Charles and Gertrude. "My name is Sean O'Neill," he said. "I'm proud to call myself a friend of Beth March. And these fine girls are my sisters Kathleen and Maggie."

"Oh," said Gertrude.

"What kind of name is Sean?" Charles asked.

" 'Tis a fine Irish name," said Sean. "I don't believe I caught yours."

"Charles," Charles said. "And this is Gertrude. Fine American names."

"That they are," said Sean. "As is the name Beth. Will you be going to school with us?"

Beth held her breath. What if Charles made a horrible joke about no dogs or Irish in his school?

But Charles just grinned. "If you're in Beth's class, we will be," he said.

"What a pretty dress," Gertrude said to Kathleen.

"Thank you," Kathleen said. "Your dress too is quite lovely."

"It's the first day of school," Beth said. "Everyone always looks her best."

"And behaves that way too, I'll wager," Sean said. "Come, Kathleen. Come, Maggie. Let's see what this fine American education will be doing for us."

"Wait for me," Beth said. Then she turned to Charles and Gertrude. "I'll see you in class," she said with a smile, and ran to catch up with her new friends.

PORTRAITS OF
LITTLE WOMEN
ACTIVITIES

BREAD PUDDING

This is a simple dessert, but it's suitable for any occasion at any time of year.

INGREDIENTS

1 cup golden raisins, dark raisins, or currants

¼ cup melted butter

6 cups coarsely crumbled biscuits or stale cubed bread (you may use French or cinnamon bread)

2 cups half-and-half

1½ cups milk

3 eggs, plus 1 egg white, slightly beaten

1½ tablespoons vanilla extract

1½ cups sugar

1 teaspoon ground cinnamon or nutmeg

Preheat oven to 325 degrees.

1. Soak raisins in warm water for at least half an hour.
2. Melt butter and pour into a 13-by-9-by-2-inch pan. Coat sides and bottom.
3. Place biscuits or stale cubed bread in a large bowl. Pour in half-and-half and milk.
4. Let mixture stand 10 minutes, then crush with hands until blended but still coarse.
5. Add eggs, egg white, vanilla, sugar, and cinnamon or nutmeg and mix well.
6. Drain raisins and add to mixture.
7. Spoon mixture into buttered pan.
8. Bake for 30 minutes or until pudding is firm. Cool completely.

Makes 12 to 15 servings.

Cut into squares and serve plain or with whipped cream or sliced fresh fruit. Can be stored in the refrigerator lightly covered.

DRIED FLOWER
BOOKMARK

Viola del pensiero

Pansy

You will treasure your dried flower bookmark for its delicate beauty and use it each time you curl up with a book.

MATERIALS

Dried flowers and leaves

Paper (heavyweight card stock or
    watercolor paper is best; color is your
    choice, but white is always nice)

Hole punch

Scissors

Fast-setting, clear-drying, water-soluble
    glue

Small, soft paintbrush

Tweezers

Waxed paper

Clear spray lacquer or hairspray

Ribbon, 1/8 yard

Drying Flowers

1. Select flat flowers (daisies, pansies, etc.) and leaves (e.g., ivy, bayberry).

2.

Place flowers and leaves between layers of wax paper, making sure the flowers and leaves don't touch each other.

3. Slip the sheets of wax paper with flowers and leaves between the pages

of a heavy book. Then place another heavy book on top and

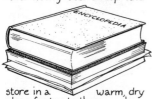

store in a warm, dry place for two to three weeks.

4.

and leaves when they fall from the wax paper. The flowers are dry freely

The flowers and leaves are dry freely when they fall from the wax paper.

Creating the Bookmark

1. Cut paper to size, then punch a hole or make a slit here

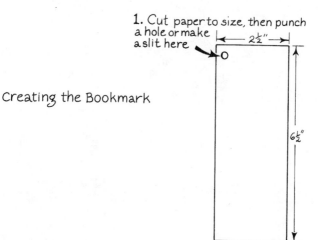

2½"

6½"

95

2.

Lay out your design, however you

like (starting with the leaves, followed by the flowers), then

Use tweezers to set the leaves in place.

use a brush to spread glue on the <u>back</u> of each leaf.

3.

Spread glue evenly and sparingly on the <u>backs</u> of the flowers, then

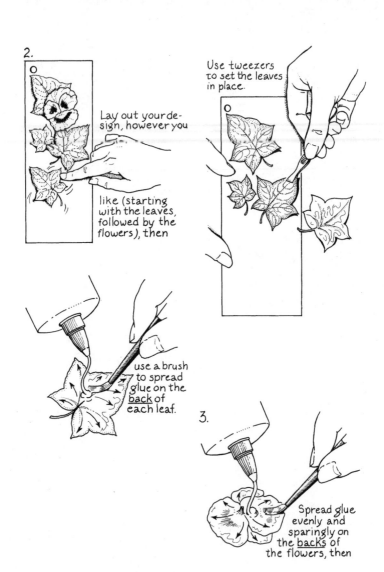

use tweezers to position the flowers.

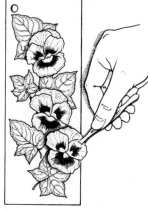

4.

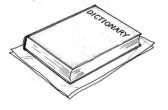

Lay wax paper over the design and place a heavy book on top for at least half an hour.

5. After the bookmark is dry, if you want to, you can write an inscription, a name, or a quote, then apply a little spray lacquer over the whole design. (Note: Spray outside or in a well-ventilated area.)

6.

Loop the ribbon through the hole and your bookmark is complete!

Your bookmark is now ready to be inserted between the pages of the next book you read.

ABOUT THE AUTHOR OF
PORTRAITS OF LITTLE WOMEN

SUSAN BETH PFEFFER is the author of both middle-grade and young adult fiction. Her middle-grade novels include *Nobody's Daughter* and its companion, *Justice for Emily*. Her highly praised *The Year Without Michael* is an ALA Best Book for Young Adults, an ALA YALSA Best of the Best, and a *Publishers Weekly* Best Book of the Year. Her novels for young adults include *Twice Taken*, *Most Precious Blood*, *About David*, and *Family of Strangers*. Susan Beth Pfeffer lives in Middletown, New York.

A WORD ABOUT
LOUISA MAY ALCOTT

LOUISA MAY ALCOTT was born in 1832 in Germantown, Pennsylvania, and grew up in the Boston-Concord area of Massachusetts. She received her early education from her father, Bronson Alcott, a renowned educator and writer, who eventually left teaching to study philosophy. To supplement the family income, Louisa worked as a teacher, a household servant, and a seamstress, and she wrote stories as well as poems for newspapers and magazines. In 1868 she published the first volume of *Little Women,* a novel about four sisters growing up in a small New England town during the Civil War. The immediate success of *Little Women* made Louisa May Alcott a celebrated writer, and the novel remains one of today's best-loved books. Alcott wrote until her death in 1888.